Spider Storch's Fumbled Field Trip

Gina Willner-Pardo
illustrated by Nick Sharratt

Albert Whitman & Company • Morton Grove, Illinois

Library of Congress Cataloging-in-Publication Data

Willner-Pardo, Gina.
Spider Storch's fumbled field trip /
by Gina Willner-Pardo ; illustrated by Nick Sharratt.
p. cm.

Summary: When his third-grade teacher sends him back to the
bus for having caused trouble while on a school field trip, Spider
makes an amazing discovery about the driver.
ISBN 0-8075-7581-x (hardcover)
ISBN 0-8075-7582-8 (paperback)
[1. School field trips—Fiction. 2. Bus drivers—Fiction.
3. Schools—Fiction. 4. Teachers—Fiction.]
I. Sharratt, Nick, ill. II. Title.
PZ7.W683675Su 1998
[Fic]—dc21
98-4909
CIP
AC

Designed by Scott Piehl.

For Sue, who taught me how to
take boys on field trips,
among other things. —G. W.-P.

For Ruth. —N. S.

Don't forget to read . . .

Spider Storch's
Teacher Torture

Spider Storch's
Carpool Catastrophe

Spider Storch's
Music Mess

by Gina Willner-Pardo

illustrated by Nick Sharratt

Contents

1
Field Trip!

"Field trips make Wednesdays feel like Saturdays," I told Zachary and Andrew. We were practicing our slam dunks at recess.

"On Saturdays all *I* do is watch cartoons," Andrew said.

"I like how everybody stares at us," Zachary said, dribbling the ball and shooting. "You'd think all those grownups had never seen a bunch of kids before."

"I like that we're going to the Institute of Life Sciences," I said. "I like the aquarium. And the alligators. The alligators are almost as cool as spiders."

Everybody knows how much I love spiders. That's my nickname: Spider. Hardly anyone calls me Joey, except for my family, and girls, and teachers.

"Wouldn't it be funny if Ms. Schmidt fell into the alligator pit?" Zachary said. Ms. Schmidt was our new third-grade teacher.

"The alligators would spit her out," Andrew said, passing me the ball.

"She probably tastes like cough syrup. Or broccoli."

"They'd scratch their throats on those fingernails," I said. "I've never seen anyone with fingernails so long. It must take a whole can of nail polish to paint them."

"That's not nail polish. It's blood," Zachary said.

"Probably from scratching out little kids' eyes," Andrew said. "I bet she eats kids' eyeballs for dinner."

Actually, Ms. Schmidt had only been our teacher for a week, since our old teacher, Ms. Mirabella, retired. We didn't really know her well enough to know what she ate for dinner. We were pretty sure, though,

11

that she slept in a coffin and could hypnotize you if you looked at her too long. You could tell. "The worst thing about field trips is all the rules," Zachary said, stealing the ball and dodging out of Andrew's way. "No running. Stay together. Tell one of the moms or dads if you have to go to the bathroom."

"The worst thing is when Mrs. Arkens is one of the moms," Andrew said.

Mrs. Arkens made you hold her hand if you weren't behaving. Nobody wanted to touch the skin of somebody else's mom.

"I know what the worst thing is," I said. "The worst thing is Mr. Bentley."

Mr. Bentley was the bus driver on field trips. He hated kids. He kept dead squirrels under the driver's seat and would make you look at them if the teacher had to send you back to the bus for not behaving. He was always telling everyone to sit down and put a sock in it. He stepped on the brakes too hard on purpose.

"They should fire Mr. Bentley," Zachary said. He went for an easy lay-up. "Somebody else could drive the bus."

"Everyone's too afraid of him to fire him. Even the moms," I said. "I heard he keeps poison under the seat."

"With the squirrels?" Andrew asked.

I nodded.

"What for?"

"You never know when you might need poison. Especially if you're crazy old Mr. Bentley."

"The best thing on field trips is to do exactly what you're supposed to do," Andrew said. "That way, you don't get stuck holding Mrs. Arkens' hand or sitting in the bus with Mr. Bentley."

I nodded, but inside I was worried. Doing exactly what I'm supposed to do isn't as easy as it sounds.

2

Boarding the Bus

The day of the field trip, Ms. Schmidt looked fancier than usual. She was wearing a dress and bright red lipstick that matched her nails. She called the roll and seemed happy that no one was absent.

"Any questions about the trip?" she asked.

Mary Grace Brennerman raised her hand. "Can I be in charge of making sure everyone stays in line?" she asked.

"*I'll* take care of that, Mary Grace," Ms. Schmidt said firmly.

Andrew and Zachary and I looked at each other. We were all relieved. Mary Grace was bad enough when she *wasn't* in charge of something.

"However, if you would like to hold my clipboard while I collect permission slips, I would appreciate it," Ms. Schmidt said.

Uh-oh. I hoped this didn't mean that Mary Grace was getting on Ms. Schmidt's good side already.

Ms. Mirabella never let Mary Grace hold her clipboard.

After she had collected permission

slips, Ms. Schmidt went over the rules. They were the same rules that Ms. Mirabella had, but Ms. Schmidt sounded more serious about them. She looked right at me when she reminded us about not wandering away from the group. I wondered if Ms. Mirabella had told her about the time we'd gone to the state capital and I'd gotten separated from the tour and accidentally set off the fire alarm.

BRRRIIINNGG!!!

FIRE ALARM

"Anyone who can't behave will return to the bus," Ms. Schmidt said. She didn't smile at all. "I'm sure that Mr. Bentley would enjoy some company."

I shuddered.

Zachary raised his hand.

"Do we have to hold hands?" he asked. "In second grade they made us hold hands."

"I don't think that's necessary," Ms. Schmidt said. "But everyone will be assigned a partner. Please stay with your partner while we tour the Institute. Don't get separated."

"Can we have two partners?" I asked. I wanted Zachary and Andrew.

"Don't call out," Ms. Schmidt said sternly. "You're in third grade now. Third-graders don't call out."

Ms. Mirabella was always telling me not to call out. She said "please," though. And she smiled when she said it.

I raised my hand. Ms. Schmidt pretended not to see me for a minute. Finally, without calling on me, she said, "Everyone will have *one* partner. A partner *I* will assign."

Rats, I thought, lowering my hand.

•

I got stuck with Regina Littlefield. Regina wasn't awful, for a girl.

"Don't even *try* to hold my hand," she said.

"Don't worry."

"If you even *touch* me, I'll sock you right in the mouth."

"I won't. I just said."

"Or breathe on me," Regina said. "If you even breathe on me, you'll be sorry."

We marched out to the bus.

 Travis Hoffberg looked worried.

"The windows don't open," he said. "I get carsick when you can't open the windows."

"Everything will be fine, Travis," Ms. Schmidt said. "You can sit up front with me."

But she didn't hug him the way Ms. Mirabella would have.

The bus door swung open. Just at that minute, Regina whispered, "I dare you to stick pencils up your nose and in your ears in front of Mr. Bentley."

Sticking pencils up your nose— even just the eraser ends—was dangerous. Even I knew that. But you can't just say no when a girl dares

you. Especially a girl with as big
a mouth as Regina.

"I don't have four
pencils," I whispered back.

Regina smiled an evil
smile. "*I* do," she said.

It took me a couple of seconds
to get all the pencils in. I had to
walk very slowly. One false move and
any one of them could have come
loose.

"I am Zubrow from Planet
Nebulon," I said in a flat, robot-y
voice. I walked with straight legs
to look even more like an alien.

In front of me, Zachary and
Andrew were cracking up.

"You look like an idiot," Regina
said.

I clomped up the steps of the bus.

The pencils were still in place.

Mr. Bentley was sitting sideways in the driver's seat. He had a big curly beard and wore a gray uniform. I had a feeling that pieces of food were stuck in that beard.

"Hey. You. What's your name?" he asked me.

I could feel Regina poking me

in the back. "I am Zubrow from Planet Nebulon," I said.

Now everyone was laughing. Everyone but Mr. Bentley and Ms. Schmidt.

"Joseph Storch! Put those pencils away!" Ms. Schmidt yelled from the front seat.

"Okay, okay," I said.

Ms. Schmidt waited until I had collected all the pencils from my face. Then she leaned forward in her seat.

"I'm warning you, Joey," she said.

She wasn't yelling anymore. I wished she were. It was scarier this way.

I looked up and saw Mr. Bentley

staring at me. He was smiling like a bad guy in the movies before he shoots you or lets the guillotine fall or tells his dog to chew off your leg.

"Mr. Storch," he said, still smiling.

"I have a feeling we're going to be seeing a lot of each other."

3

The Institute
of Life Sciences

The Institute of Life Sciences was
in a huge stone building with pillars
and big steps. It looked like someplace
a president might live, except for the
fake whale hanging from the ceiling.

The alligators were in the first room, in an indoor pond with some turtles.

"What are the differences between alligators and crocodiles?" Ms. Schmidt asked.

Mary Grace raised her hand and moaned, "Ooh, ooh," like she really knew the answer. But Ms. Schmidt called on Suzanne Mayberry.

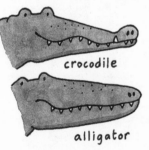

crocodile

alligator

"Crocodiles have pointy snouts," Suzanne said. "Alligator snouts are broad and flat."

"Very good, Suzanne," Ms. Schmidt said.

The alligators looked cool, but they weren't very interesting to watch. I kept wondering if one of them would eat a turtle, but they all just lay there.

We walked into another room with big glass tanks and cages.

"SNAKES!" Zachary and Andrew and I yelled at the same time.

"Boys!" Ms. Schmidt turned around and gave us a dirty look. "Keep your voices down!"

I felt a hand on my shoulder.

"I'm watching you, Joey," Mrs. Arkens said.

"You'd better be careful," Regina whispered.

We walked past boas and garters and diamondbacks and even a giant python.

"Snakes are disgusting," Mary Grace said.

I imagined the giant python having Mary Grace for lunch. I wondered if he would shred her into little pieces or swallow her whole. As long as she was in one piece, I had a feeling you'd still be able to hear her yakking.

We looked at newts and monitors and toads and frogs. I hoped there'd

Yak yak yak...

be tomato frogs, which Ms. Mirabella used to keep in a terrarium on her desk, but there weren't. I felt a little sad inside. I'd forgotten about those tomato frogs. I sure missed them.

"Ms. Schmidt?" Andrew asked. "Where are all the fish?"

"Just through this door," Ms. Schmidt said.

It was dark in the next room. The only lights were in the tanks. Some were small and full of tiny, bright fish. They swam in groups, first one way, then another. They always stuck together.

"How do they all know how to turn together?" Regina asked.

"It's a mystery," Ms. Schmidt said.

"What if one fish smells or has bad

breath?" I asked. "Can the other fish take a vote and throw him out of the group?"

"It's called a school, Joey," Ms. Schmidt said. "And fish don't get thrown out of it."

"No matter what?"

"Fish don't even have noses," Mary Grace said.

"No," Ms. Schmidt said. "But they *do* have two nostrils on each side of their heads. And an organ called the olfactory rosette helps them to detect smells in their environments."

Ha, ha, I thought, making a face at Mary Grace. It's a good thing she and I aren't fish, I thought. I'd be stuck with her all the time. At least, being people, I only had to be around her for six hours a day.

Some of the tanks were huge. They were full of different kinds of fish: catfish and  barracudas and carp and bass and pike. There were sea anemones and coral and starfish and urchins.

"They look like plants!" I said.

"But they're animals," Ms. Schmidt said. "Many animals that live underwater need oxygen dissolved in seawater to survive. Underwater plants need carbon dioxide."

"Whoa!" Andrew said. He had moved ahead and was looking at the next tank. It was full of big fish. One was huge: brown and ugly, with mean eyes.

"What is that?" Zachary asked.

Regina and I read the plaque on the wall.

"A sturgeon," I said. "It's been in this aquarium for fifty-five years."

"That fish is older than my grandpa," Regina said.

We watched as the sturgeon circled the tank. All the other fish looked like they were trying to get out of its way.

"Like Jeremy Bettencourt at recess," I said.

Jeremy Bettencourt was in the fourth grade. He was always trying to steal the basketball from the third-graders.

"Every summer we go camping at Gold Feather Lake," I said. "I wonder if there are fish that big swimming around out there. I've never seen any."

"They probably stay near the bottom of the lake," Mary Grace said. "They're probably more afraid of you than you are of them."

"Who says I'm afraid of them? I'm not afraid of some dumb old sturgeon," I said. "I'd just like to know if they're out there, is all. I don't want to step on one by accident."

"Yeah, right," Mary Grace said. She looked over at Ms. Schmidt, who was reading a plaque about eels and not paying any attention to us. "Joey's afraid of a fi-ish," she sang in a whispery voice.

I was about to shove Mary Grace up against the wall when I felt Andrew grab my arm.

"Careful, Spider," he said. "Remember Mr. Bentley."

I stopped and took a deep breath.

"Thanks," I said. I saw Mrs. Arkens looking at me.

I thought of two things. The first was that Sturgeon Breath would be a good nickname for Mary Grace. The second was that it didn't seem fair, that fish being so crummy-looking. Maybe it was the coolest

fish in the whole Institute and nobody
even knew, on account of it looked so
scary.

4

Tidepool Tumble

After a snack, Ms. Schmidt led us
to the Touch and Feel Tidepool.

"You may pick up and hold the
creatures that live in the tidepool,"
she said. "You must be gentle. These
are living things."

I raised my hand. "Maybe this isn't such a good idea," I said.

"What makes you say that, Joey?" Ms. Schmidt asked.

"Well ..." I knew how some kids could be. They were always thinking it was funny to kill spiders. "Maybe it would be better if we just looked."

A few of the girls giggled. Mary Grace raised her hand.

"Joey's afraid of touching a sea cucumber!" she said.

"Why don't you *sit* on a sea cucumber?" I said. I wasn't thinking. I just said it. I always do that: talk without thinking. It's my worst quality.

"Joey?" Ms. Schmidt looked very irritated.

The class got very quiet.

"Yes, Ms. Schmidt?" I said.

Ms. Schmidt folded her arms. "This is your last chance," she said. "Don't blow it."

Zachary and Andrew tried to be nice.

"We know you didn't mean it," Zachary said. "We know you would never want Mary Grace to sit on a sea cucumber."

"The sea cucumber would get smushed," Andrew said.

I nodded. "You know how I am when Mary Grace says something stupid," I said. "I can't control myself."

The tidepool was like an indoor pond with a wall around it. You could lean over and put your hands in the

38

water. A lady in a uniform was standing nearby and watching all the kids to make sure no one threw any of the animals around or spit in the water or started a splash fight. I was glad she was there. Kids could be rough on animals and not even mean it.

"Hey, look! A starfish!" Regina cried.

"Be careful with that!" I said. Regina was waving it around like a flag. How come there was no grownup around yelling when you needed one?

"Look at all its suckers," Regina said.

I looked. It was pretty amazing. Still ... "Why don't you put it back in the water?" I said.

"Quit telling me what to do," Regina said.

I made myself think. I made sure my voice wasn't shouting. I kept my hands to myself.

"Holding them out of the water makes them stressed," I said quietly. "I read that somewhere."

Regina put the starfish down gently on a rock. "I didn't mean to hurt it," she said.

I felt kind of bad. I didn't say anything about being sorry, though. I didn't want anyone thinking I liked Regina. Instead I said, "Look! I'm a blowfish!" and puffed out my cheeks and crossed my eyes.

Regina laughed, and I felt better.

All of a sudden I heard Mary Grace say, "Oooh!" She was standing on the other side of the tide-pool. She was holding a giant sea cucumber. But I knew Mary Grace. She hated touching things that were wet and slimy. Hated even thinking about them. Once in first grade, I told the class how a slug had gotten into our dishwasher, and Mary Grace had to go to the principal's office to lie down. I *knew* that "oooh" was a bad sign. I knew Mary Grace was going to drop that sea cucumber.

The next few seconds were kind of a blur. I don't really remember how it happened. I know that Ms. Schmidt

and the lady in the uniform were
talking and not paying any attention
to Mary Grace. Zachary
yelled something like,
"No, Spider!" and
Andrew grabbed my
arm. Everyone was
screaming.

But the next thing I
really remember was standing in the
middle of the Touch and Feel Tidepool,
trying to get to Mary Grace before she
dropped the sea cucumber.

"Joseph Storch!" Ms. Schmidt cried.
All the screaming had finally gotten
her attention. "What are you doing
in the tidepool?"

"Young man!" the lady in uniform
yelled. "Don't move a muscle! You
might step on something!"

I hadn't thought of that. I froze and looked down. Was I squishing a sea cucumber and not even realizing it? Cold water was seeping through the bottoms of my sneakers. I felt horrible, and also like a huge idiot.

The lady in uniform ran to the edge of the tidepool and held out her hand. "Hold on to me," she said, "and watch where you put your feet."

I looked over at Ms. Schmidt. Her eyes were little black slits.

"Mary Grace was going to drop the sea cucumber!" I explained.

"I *didn't* drop it," Mary Grace said. "See? I set him down just the way you're supposed to."

I looked to where she pointed. The sea cucumber looked okay. Kind of like a big, flat pickle lying under the water.

"Well, you *almost* dropped it," I yelled.

Ms. Schmidt held up her hand. "Silence!" she said.

I kept my eyes on the water as I took careful steps to the side of the tidepool. Everyone was laughing and pointing at me. The lady in the uniform shook her head as I stepped out of the tidepool.

"I'm afraid I can't have you walking through the Institute in those clothes," she said.

I looked down. My pants were plastered to my legs. I was dripping water everywhere.

I was about to ask if anyone had an extra pair of pants when Ms. Schmidt said, "Oh, don't worry. Mr. Storch won't be accompanying us on the rest of our tour."

Everyone stopped laughing and pointing. It was so quiet that I wasn't sure anyone was even breathing. Mary Grace looked too shocked even to stick out her tongue. I think she actually felt sorry for me.

"Joey will be drying off in the bus," Ms. Schmidt said.

5

Lunch on the Bus

Ms. Schmidt stayed with the rest
of the class while Mrs. Arkens took me
out to the bus. Her sneakers squeaked
on the black marble floors. I tried to
take my hand out of hers, but she held
on tight. My fingers felt hot and
sweaty. I thought I might throw up.

I felt like a criminal on the way to
the firing squad.

When we got to the parking lot,
I looked over at her. It felt important
to tell the truth.

"I didn't mean to make a mess,"
I said. "I was just worried about the
sea—"

The bus door hissed open.

"Well, well, well," Mr. Bentley
said. He smiled. I think he
was missing some teeth. "Mr.
Storch. What a surprise."

My heart was bouncing

around in my chest like a rubber ball.

"Mr. Bentley," Mrs. Arkens said. "It seems that Mr. Storch and I will be joining you for lunch today."

"The more the merrier," Mr. Bentley said.

We climbed onto the bus. I tried to follow Mrs. Arkens down the aisle. She was creepy, but at least she didn't make you look at dead squirrels.

Mrs. Arkens shook her head. "I plan to spend lunchtime reading," she said. "You may sit up front with Mr. Bentley." She pointed to a seat and waited until I took it. Then she walked to the back of the bus.

Mr. Bentley and I just sat there. Neither of us said a word. Mr. Bentley leaned back in the driver's seat with his arms folded over his stomach and watched the cars driving through the parking lot. A little radio propped up against the dashboard was playing country music. It was so quiet I could barely hear it.

I smelled something. It was hard to describe. It might have been rotting flesh. I wasn't sure.

Mr. Bentley must have heard me sniffing. He turned around.

"What's your problem?" he asked.

"What do you mean?" I said. But I couldn't help adding, "What's that smell?"

"What smell?"

"I don't know. *That* smell."

"I don't smell anything," Mr. Bentley said. He stretched a little in his seat. "Maybe it's *you*."

"*Me*?" Did I smell? "Why would it be me?"

"You smell like a wet dog," he said.

"I can't help it," I said. "I fell in the tidepool!"

"Sure you did," Mr. Bentley said. He turned back to the steering wheel.

"I *did*!" I yelled. I was scaring myself a little. Usually I didn't yell at grownups, except once in a while my parents. But this guy was getting on my nerves. I didn't want him thinking I'd wet my pants or something.

"Mary Grace Brennerman was about to drop a sea cucumber, and

I felt sorry for it and tried to catch it, and before I knew it I was standing in the tidepool. And Ms. Schmidt was mad because I got all wet and because she thought I was misbehaving, and she made me sit out here," I said. "And that's the truth," I added.

Mr. Bentley turned around in his seat. "Is the sea cucumber okay?" he asked.

"I think so," I said.

Mr. Bentley nodded. "Good," he said. He turned back in his seat.

"No offense intended," he said.

We sat without talking for a few minutes. I stared at the back of Mr. Bentley's head. Grownups didn't apologize very often. Never to me. I didn't know what to think.

I was starting to get hungry. "Can

I eat my lunch?" I asked.

"Be my guest," Mr. Bentley said.

I opened my lunch bag. Mom had packed a ham sandwich, a sack of chips, some chocolate-chip cookies, an orange, and a box of apple juice.

"Rats," I said.

Mr. Bentley turned around again.

"What's the problem?"

"I got a crummy lunch," I said.

Mr. Bentley leaned over to look in my lunch bag.

"Let's see," he said. I opened my bag wide. Mr. Bentley peered inside. "Are those cookies homemade?" he asked.

"No," I said. "My mom got them at the store. In a bag."

Mr. Bentley seemed to be thinking. "I'm a big fan of chocolate-chip cookies," he said. "I'll trade you for them."

This was weird. Grownups didn't trade for cookies.

"What do you have?" I asked.

"A chocolate cupcake. And some olives."

"Black or green?"

"Black."

My favorite.

"The cupcake and the olives for the cookies, then," I said.

"No way," Mr. Bentley said. "Who do you think you're kidding?"

I settled for half a cupcake and five olives. You could say a lot about Mr. Bentley, but he could spot a lousy trade a mile away.

When he opened his lunch bag to get the cupcake and the olives, the funny smell I'd noticed got stronger.

"That smell's coming from your lunch!" I said.

Mr. Bentley smiled. "Oh, that. It's a liverwurst-and-onion sandwich," he said. "I eat it every day. I don't even notice the smell anymore."

"Liverwurst?" I said. "Is that made from guts?"

Mr. Bentley nodded. "From pork liver. It's delicious. You want some?"

"No, thanks." I thought of something. "I bet girls hate liverwurst."

"I bet you're right." Mr. Bentley split his cupcake in two. He handed

me one half. "They don't know what
they're missing," he said.

"It might be a good thing to carry
around," I said. I imagined the look on
Mary Grace's face when I told her I
had a pig-guts sandwich in my lunch.

"I suppose it could come in handy,"
Mr. Bentley said.

We ate without talking for a while.

After he finished his lunch, Mr.
Bentley balled up his lunch sack and

tossed it into a plastic garbage bag hanging off the dashboard. Then he leaned down and grabbed something under his seat.

Uh-oh, I thought. "What's that?" I asked.

I must have sounded scared.

"What do you think?" Mr. Bentley said. "Dead squirrels?"

I could feel my jaw drop open.

Mr. Bentley said, "I know what kids say."

"You do?"

"Sure." He shrugged. "I don't mind. It's kind of funny, really."

"Boy," I said. "If people were saying I kept dead squirrels under my seat and I didn't, I'd want them to know about it."

"Maybe," he said. "Or maybe you'd think it made you sound more interesting than just being some guy who drives a bus."

I'd never thought of that.

"So what *is* under your seat?" I asked.

"My chess set,"  he said. "Want to play?"

I shook my head. "Chess is for the

57

smart kids," I said.

"Oh, you're smart enough to play chess," Mr. Bentley said.

"I don't know," I said.

"I can tell about these things," Mr. Bentley said. "Trust me."

I watched as he opened the board and set up all the pieces. Once I looked toward the back of the bus. I wanted Mrs. Arkens to know that Mr. Bentley thought I was smart enough to play chess. But she had fallen asleep. Her head was resting against the window, and she was snoring in a way that made her lips flap open and closed.

I turned back to Mr. Bentley.

"I don't know where everything goes," I said.

"That's okay. I'll show you," Mr. Bentley said.

6

Scary Mr. Bentley

Chess was fun. Mr. Bentley showed me how to move all the pieces. We played two games. He won once and so did I. He might have let me win, though.

While we played, we talked. Mr. Bentley said that being a bus driver was all right. But sometimes it got boring just driving places. When he was younger, he wanted to be a teacher. He still thought about it sometimes.

"You'd have been a good teacher," I said. "Anyone who can teach me how to play chess is a good teacher."

"Thanks," Mr. Bentley said. He looked like he really meant it.

Playing chess, Mr. Bentley and I really got to know each other. I told him how red-leg spiders tear off their prickly hairs and throw them at attackers. He told me how once he had to clean throw-up off the back seat three times in two days.

I forgot how all the kids were so afraid of him.

We finished our last game just as the third-graders filed out the front door of the Institute of Life Sciences. I felt sorry that everyone was coming back. I had a feeling that Mr. Bentley was full of good stories.

"One thing, Joey," he said just before he swung the door open.

Somehow, I already knew what he was going to ask me.

"I won't tell anybody about the chess set," I said.

Mr. Bentley smiled. "I like the kids thinking I'm kind of scary," he said.

"It helps keep them in line. A teacher taught me that. Good teachers know that sometimes it helps to be a little scary."

"I guess I see," I said. "If I wasn't a little bit scared of teachers, I'd probably never hear a word they said."

"Thanks for understanding," Mr. Bentley said.

I wanted to thank Mr. Bentley for teaching me to play chess. For thinking I was smart enough to learn. I wanted to tell him that I was glad he was a bus driver, even if it was a boring job. But there wasn't much time. The kids were almost back.

Just before the door swung open, I said, "When no one's around, you can call me Spider."

"Spider," Mr. Bentley said. "I'll remember that."

He wasn't smiling—the kids were close enough to see through the door windows—but he said it in a smiley way.

7

The World's Meanest Teacher

"Well?" Zachary hissed as he slid into the seat next to me.

"Well what?"

Andrew plunked down in front of us.

"Was it awful?"

I didn't want to lie to my friends.

But it was funny. Now Mr. Bentley was sort of a friend.

"I can't talk about it," I said.

"Wow," Zachary said. "Did he show you the squirrels?"

I closed my eyes and sighed.

"If I told you," I said, "you'd never believe it."

Zachary and Andrew looked impressed.

"At least you weren't bored," Andrew said. "This was the most boring field trip ever."

"I thought the Institute was cool," I said.

"It was," Zachary said. "Only we never got to see any of it. After you left, we had lunch. Then Ms. Schmidt handed out dittos and made us answer questions about all the

66

animals we'd seen."

"It was just like school," Andrew said. "Only without a comfortable place to sit down."

"Ms. Schmidt is mean," Zachary said. "She said anyone who didn't finish filling out the ditto has to do it for homework tonight."

"I hate homework," Andrew said. He sighed.

"Ms. Schmidt is probably the world's meanest teacher. Not as mean as Mr. Bentley, probably. But almost."

He stopped talking as Ms. Schmidt walked up the aisle.

"How was lunch, Joey?" she said.

"Okay," I said.

She had a funny look on her face.
Not really a smile. But close.

"Next time maybe you'll enjoy the
tidepool from dry land," she said.

Ms. Mirabella would have said it in
almost exactly the same way.

turtle

sea urchin

newt

catfish

coral

frog

boa

chameleon

carp

monitor

star fish

bass

gecko

sea anenome

pike

toad